KING
FOR A
DAY

by Rukhsana Khan

illustrations by Christiane Krömer

LEE & LOW BOOKS INC. ✦ NEW YORK

Basant (ba-SANT): spring kite festival celebrated all across South Asia; see last page of book for more information

Insha Allah (in-sheh AL-lah): Arabic phrase meaning "If God wills"

Malik (MAW-lik): Arabic name meaning "king"

Text copyright © 2014 by Rukhsana Khan

Illustrations copyright © 2014 by Christiane Krömer

LEE & LOW BOOKS Inc., 95 Madison Avenue, New York, NY 10016, leeandlow.com

A version of this story, entitled *King of the Skies*, was published in Canada in 2001 by North Winds Press, a division of Scholastic Canada Ltd.

Manufactured in China by Toppan

Book design by Kimi Weart

Book production by The Kids at Our House

The text is set in Minion

The illustrations are rendered in mixed-media collage

(hc) 10 9 8 7 6 5 4

(pb) 10 9 8 7 6 5

First Edition

Library of Congress Cataloging-in-Publication Data

Khan, Rukhsana.

King for a day / by Rukhsana Khan ; illustrations by Christiane Krömer. — First edition.

pages cm

Summary: "Even though he is confined to a wheelchair, a Pakistani boy tries to capture the most kites during Basant, the annual spring kite festival, and become 'king' for the day. Includes an afterword about the Basant festival"—Provided by publisher.

ISBN 978-1-60060-659-5 (hc)   ISBN 978-1-64379-056-5 (pb)

[1. Basant Festival—Fiction. 2. Kites—Fiction. 3. Wheelchairs—Fiction. 4. People with disabilities—Fiction. 5. Pakistan—Fiction.]

I. Krömer, Christiane, illustrations. II. Title.

PZ7.K52654Ki 2013   [E]—dc23   2013007506

For my father, Muhammad Anwar Khan,
a wise "king" (for more than a day)
—*R.K.*

For Tomar Levine, the godmother
of books and dreams
—*C.K.*

Basant is the most exciting day of the year! With feasts and music and parties, people celebrate the arrival of spring. And many will make their way to the rooftops of Lahore to test their skills in kite-flying battles.

I'm up early. My brother and sister arrive, still rubbing sleep from their eyes.

My brother asks, "Malik, is that all you made?"

My sister says, "How can you be king of Basant with only one kite?"

"It's called Falcon. *Insha Allah*, it will be fast enough."

I send my brother many blocks downwind so he can catch the kites I will set free.

There's the bully next door. Ha! It's time to make him pay for hitting me and throwing stones at my sister. I'll get back at him with Falcon.

The bully shouts at us, calling my sister a bad name.

My sister yells right back, but when she turns around, I can see she is hurt inside.

The breeze lifts the bully's huge kite. His kite is so big I nickname it Goliath. It must have cost a fortune.

Falcon is small, built for speed.

I let out enough of my special string for my sister to carry Falcon to the edge of the roof.

"Don't step on the tails!" I cry. "Don't rip them!"

On the count of three, my sister jumps. I tug on the string. Falcon leaps into the sky.

I'm ready to attack.

I work my string, dipping Falcon so it circles Goliath.

Because it is so big, Goliath is slow.

My kite string rubs the bully's kite string. *Snip*. I have sliced it. Goliath flies free, and the bully's string drops from the sky like a fishing line with nothing on the hook.

The bully picks up his other kite. A smaller, faster kite. He gets it climbing on the rising currents of air until it's almost as high as Falcon.

I take a deep breath, bracing myself.

The bully's kite circles, trying to trap Falcon. I move away, watching closely for the next attack. The bully pulls his kite left.

Quickly I pull down as hard as I can, sending Falcon into a steep dive.

"Let up, Malik!" my sister yells. "You're going to crash."

Just before Falcon hits the rooftop, I pull it up and around several times, snagging the bully's string so he cannot get it free.

I reel in the bully's kite so my sister can grab it.

The bully's done. He has no more kites. He storms downstairs.

I move on to other kites. It's easy for Falcon to pluck them from the sky as if it really is a bird of prey.

Big kites, little kites, fancy and plain. Even kites made of old newspapers. Sometimes I catch them in groups. Making wide circles around clusters of kites, Falcon slashes through their strings.

For a while the kites fly where the wind carries them. When they land, they'll belong to whoever finds them. But at least they will have tasted freedom.

Insha Allah, I really am king of Basant today!

Throughout the day, my brother brings
some of the kites I have freed up to the
roof. Among them is Goliath. My sister
stacks them in a pile.

Sometimes loose kites float close
enough for me to catch. Falcon tangles
their strings, and I draw them in.

My sister catches some too. She uses a
long bamboo pole topped with thorns.
If I am king, she is queen of Basant.

At the end of the day we have a big pile of kites. I choose the two I want. Then my brother and sister get their picks.

After they have chosen, they start back downstairs. My sister says, "Malik? You coming?"

"Not yet."

The sun is setting on a magnificent day. I want to stay up here to watch, to feel the cool breeze. I want to make my day last a little longer.

Suddenly I hear yelling from below.

The bully pushes a young girl to the ground. Then he grabs her kite and runs into his house.

The girl gets to her feet. Sobbing, she heads down the alley trailing the kite string behind her.

Something makes me pick up Goliath and drop it over the side of the roof. It floats, slicing the air side to side, to land close beside her.

The crying stops. The girl picks up Goliath.

I duck just as she looks up to see where it came from.

When I look again, she's dancing along. Then she rounds the corner. She's gone.

One by one the stars come out till they shine down like a million jeweled kites. My day is done. I am no longer king of Basant.

It's time to go downstairs and join my brother and sister. We have many stories to tell of Falcon's triumphs. And tomorrow I will start designing a new kite, an even better kite, for next Basant when, *Insha Allah*, I will be king again.

About Basant

There is something glorious about going up on a roof and releasing kites in the air. Even more thrilling is doing battle with them! In early spring, when the chill of winter has fled from the ancient city of Lahore, Pakistan, and light breezes carry the scent of flowers, it is time for Basant, the annual kite festival.

Basant started many years ago with the Hindu celebration that marked the end of cool weather and the beginning of warm weather. With time, Basant became a celebration that crossed religious and cultural boundaries. People from inside and outside Pakistan flocked to Lahore to watch or participate in the kite battles. Many kite enthusiasts spent weeks preparing for the festival, practicing their flying skills by waging mock battles.

The festival begins on the night before Basant. Huge spotlights are perched on rooftops so people can see, and white kites are flown because white shows up best in the night sky. The next day, people bring out their colorful kites. Shouts and cheers, drumming and bugle blasts create a festive mood. Everywhere there are feasts and parties. Women dress in bright colors, often wearing yellow or green to represent spring. Toward the end of the day, people bring out even larger kites, and at night there are fireworks to symbolize all the kite battles.

Traditionally kite strings were coated with powdered glass so they would be sharp enough to cut through other kite strings. Later, metal strings were also used. Unfortunately the sharp strings sometimes injured people and cut electrical wires. In recent years, kite flying and the celebration of Basant in Lahore were banned for safety reasons and for security concerns due to orthodox religious opposition. But many people are trying to revive the festival while ensuring better safety. It will certainly lift the spirits of the people of Lahore to see the sky once again filled with brilliant color and drama.